Agapanthus Hum

and the Angel Hoot

For my wonderful daughter Judith Cowley,
who was my own Agapanthus Hum

—J.C.

For Patti

—J.P.

Agapanthus Hum
and the
Angel Hoot

Joy Cowley

author of Mrs. Wishy-Washy

Pictures by Jennifer Plecas

PHILOMEL BOOKS

Table of Contents

Chapter One

Agapanthus Hum
had a woggly front tooth.
One day, it fell out
on a bite of carrot,
and dropped like a pearl
into her lap.

"Mommy! Daddy! Come and see!"

Good little Mommy
and good little Daddy
came running.
"Well done, Agapanthus!"
cried good little Mommy.

"You'll soon have a big tooth
there, honey," good little Daddy said.

The new tooth had already begun.
Agapanthus could feel it,
hard at the top of the tooth hole.
A hum started inside her,
and her arms and legs
went all whizzy.
She twirled into the bathroom
to look in the mirror.

3

In the rush of things,
she knocked her glasses
clean off her face.
But they were all right,
because they landed
on a thick, soft towel.

Good little Mommy
put the glasses back
on Agapanthus Hum's nose.
Now Agapanthus could see
the hole in her smile.

"Oh!" she cried.
"Congratulations, me!
I am growing up!"

Chapter Two

The next day, Agapanthus
and her dog, Major Bark,
were doing a bumblebee dance
around the garden.
Agapanthus was humming
a good buzzing song.

When she came to the roses,
she opened her lips
to blow the bumblebee hum
through her tooth tunnel.
What a surprise!

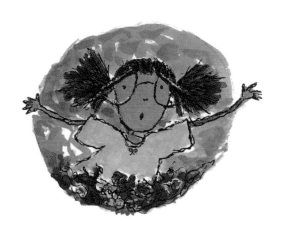

It did not come out as a hum
but as a long, shrill note,
like the whistle of a train.

Too-oo-oo-oot!

Major stopped so quickly
he fell over himself.

Agapanthus could not believe
that the noise had come
from her own tooth tunnel.

She did it again,
and again.

Major sat down,
put his head back,
and howled.
Ow-ow-ow-ow-ow!

Chapter Three

Faster than any bumblebee,
Agapanthus flew back to the house.
"Mommy! Daddy! I can whistle!"

Too-oo-oo-oot!

"Why, Agapanthus Hum,"
said good little Daddy.
"That is not a whistle.
That is an angel hoot."

"An angel what?"
Agapanthus asked.

"Hoot," said good little Daddy.
"It is how angels call to each other
on a wild and windy day."
He winked to let her know
that it might be slightly true.

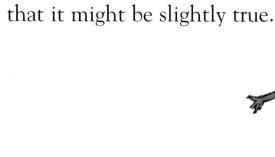

Agapanthus was so pleased
that she blew again,
puffing out her cheeks
to make a loud blast.

At once, Major's head went back
and he howled like a wolf.

Good little Mommy laughed.
"What a performance!
You whistle and Major sings.
The famous hoot-and-howl act."

"Do we really sound good?"
asked Agapanthus.

"Like two angels," her father said,
winking again.

Chapter Four

When Orville came over to play,
Agapanthus showed him
her baby tooth.

"It looks just like a pearl," she said.

"Nah," said Orville.
"More like a lemon seed."

Agapanthus put her tooth back in her pocket
and pushed her glasses up on her nose.
"Have you got a woggly tooth?"

With his fingers, Orville felt
all the way around his mouth.

"I've got four whole teeth
just about woggly," he said.

"Listen to this," said Agapanthus,
and she blew through the tooth tunnel.
The noise screeched through the garden,
and Major started howling,
his nose to the sky.
Orville stared. "How'd you do that?"

Agapanthus showed him.
"It's called an angel hoot."

Orville tried several times,
then shrugged and said,
"I can quack like a duck.
I'm very expert at quacking."

"I know," said Agapanthus.
"But you can only do an angel hoot
when you have a tooth hole."

"I can walk on my hands,"
said Orville. "I know heaps
of fantastic card tricks.
I can make my ears wriggle."

"When your tooth comes out,
you will be able to do it, too,"
Agapanthus said.

Orville flipped over on his hands
and started to walk across the lawn.
"Nah," he said in an upside-down voice.
"Angel hoots are not my thing."

Chapter Five

Agapanthus wanted to do
the hoot-and-howl act
for her class Show-and-Tell,
but good little Mommy said
that Miss Ryan might not want
to have a dog at school.

"Everyone loves Major Bark,"
said Agapanthus. "I love him.
Miss Ryan loves him.
All the kids love him.
The principal loves him."

"I know what we can do,"
said good little Mommy.
"I can go with you to school.
When Show-and-Tell is over,
I will bring Major back home."

Major squeaked, and swept
the floor with his tail.
He had been to school before.
He knew what it meant.

"I will call Miss Ryan right now,"
said good little Mommy.

Chapter Six

Agapanthus showed the class
her little pearl tooth
and the hole in her smile.

Major followed his nose,
sniff, sniff, sniff,
past Miss Ryan's shoes,
across the rug, to the bookcase.
On top of the bookcase
was the wire cage
that held the class's pet rat.

Agapanthus told everybody
about the angel hoot.
"It's what angels do
when the wind is blowing
their feathers about."

One of the girls said,
"Angels don't have feathers.
They're not chickens."

"They have feathers
on their wings," said Orville.

"Angels don't have wings,"
the girl replied. "They're invisible.
They're made of air."

Major stood on his hind
legs to sniff the rat cage.
He growled softly
between his teeth.

Orville got up from the mat
and stamped his feet together.
"Angels have wings.
End of discussion," he said.

But everyone knew that Orville
was Agapanthus's friend,
so that did not count
as much as a button.

An argument about angels' wings
filled the classroom.
Miss Ryan clapped her hands
and cried, "Children! Children!"
while Major tried to chew
the wire on the rat's cage.

The shouting grew so loud
that Agapanthus's talk
got lost like a raisin
in a pudding.

She took a deep breath
and puffed out her cheeks.
Then she blew
through her tooth gap.

Too-oo-oo-oot!

The noise stopped.
The boys and girls stared,
their mouths and eyes
as round as doughnuts.

Major tumbled backward
and rolled on the floor.

Agapanthus whistled again.

Too-oo-oo-oot!

Major sat up straight.
He shut his eyes,
pointed his nose in the air,
and howled. Ow-ow-ow-ow!

33

Everyone sat absolutely still.

Then a boy said,

"Awesome!"

"Thank you, Agapanthus,"
said Miss Ryan. "That was truly—"

"An angel hoot, Miss Ryan,"
said Orville.

"I was going to say 'amazing,'"
Miss Ryan replied.
She grabbed Major by the collar
and dragged him away
from the rat cage.

"Do it again! Do it again!"
the children called.

"Just one more time," said Miss Ryan,
holding Major's collar.

Agapanthus pushed her glasses
back up on her nose
and breathed in.
Major raised his head.

Too-oo-oo-oot!

Ow-ow-ow-ow-ow!

It was the best hoot-and-howl yet.

The whole class clapped,
Miss Ryan smiled,
and good little Mommy
watched through the doorway.

Agapanthus was so pleased
that she stood on one foot
and did a small whizzy dance,
waving her arms like wings
on a wild and windy day.

Chapter Seven

Orville went away
on vacation for three weeks.
When he came back,
he called Agapanthus.
"Listen to this!" he said,
and he did an angel hoot
over the phone.

"Do it again!" She laughed,
holding the phone
away from her ear.

Too-oo-oo-oot!

"We can be a threesome,"
said Orville. "You know,
you, me, and Major,
the famous hoot-and-howl act."

Agapanthus Hum
twisted the phone cord
around her fingers.

"Orville, I can't do angel hoots
anymore," she told him.
"My big tooth has grown
over the hole."

"It has?" Orville was quiet
for a moment. Then he said,
"Is it okay if I come over
and borrow Major?"

Agapanthus said,
"Sure you can, Orville.
You're our friend."

Good little Mommy
came into the room.
"Is that Orville?" she asked.
"Did you tell him your news?"

Agapanthus remembered
and let go of the phone cord.
She jumped up and down so fast
that her glasses fell off one ear
and slipped down her nose.

"Orville! Guess what!" she cried.
"I've got two more woggly teeth."

Dear readers,

I enjoy Agapanthus because she is a fizzy whizzy person with ideas that dance to the music of her humming. Are you like that? Do your arms and legs sometimes jive around by themselves? Do you sing fizzy whizzy made-up songs when no one is listening? What about angel hoots? Can you whistle through your teeth like Agapanthus?

Agapanthus loves stories so much that sometimes she hugs books. Have you ever hugged a favorite book?

I will tell you a secret. Even old, old authors like me hug their favorite books.

With love,
Joy Cowley

P.S. Agapanthus says that angels wear eyeglasses so they can see how beautiful the world is.

PATRICIA LEE GAUCH, EDITOR.

PHILOMEL BOOKS,
a division of Penguin Putnam Books for Young Readers,
345 Hudson Street, New York, NY 10014.
Philomel Books, Reg. U.S. Pat. & Tm. Off. Published simultaneously in Canada.
Manufactured in China by South China Printing Co. Ltd.
The text is set in Goudy Old Style.
Library of Congress Cataloging-in-Publication Data
Cowley, Joy. Agapanthus Hum and the angel hoot / Joy Cowley ;
pictures by Jennifer Plecas. p. cm.
Summary: When she loses a tooth, Agapanthus discovers that she can make
an angel hoot by blowing through the hole in her smile.
[1. Teeth—Fiction.] I. Plecas, Jennifer, ill. II. Title.
PZ7.C8375 Ae 2003 [E]—dc21 98-11011
ISBN 0-399-23344-X
3 5 7 9 10 8 6 4 2